A SURPRISE FOR FI

MO

BUZZ

SNICKER

RIFF

WHEEZY

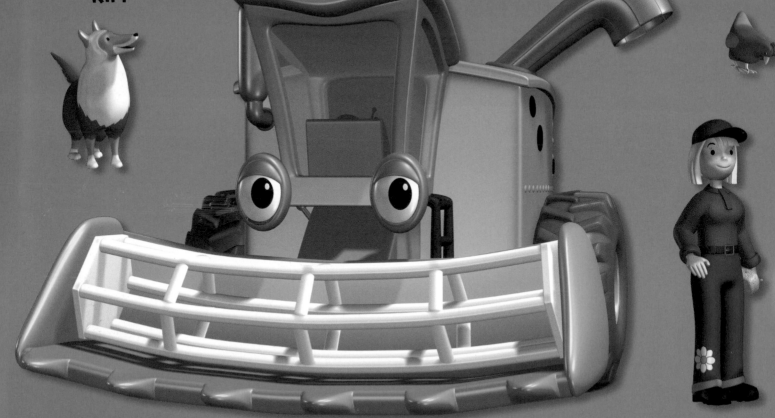

FARMER FI

THE SHEEP

PURDEY

WACK

BACH

THE HENS

REV

MATT

TOM

WINNIE

First published in Great Britain by HarperCollins Children's Books in 2004

1 3 5 7 9 10 8 6 4 2

ISBN: 0-00-718901-X

Text adapted from the original script by Mark Holloway

The Contender Entertainment Group
48 Margaret Street, London, W1W 8SE

Tractor Tom © Contender Ltd 2002

Printed and bound in China

A SURPRISE FOR FI

Collins

An imprint of HarperCollins*Publishers*

It was a very special day at Springhill Farm –
Farmer Fi's birthday!

"Happy birthday!" said Matt. "When does
the party start?"

"Not until I find Riff," worried Fi. "She's
disappeared!"

Farmer Fi's sheepdog, Riff, had gone missing.
Tractor Tom wanted to help find her, so he and
Farmer Fi went off to search.

When they had gone, Matt started to make plans...

"Fi hasn't got time to arrange a birthday party, so we'll have to do it for her. Right, first job is to make a cake. You all know what to do!"

Buzz brought flour.
There were eggs from the hens.
Mo carried a pail of milk.
At last, Matt put the cake into the oven in Fi's kitchen.

Tractor Tom and Farmer Fi were busy searching
for Riff.

"Baa-ba-ba-ba-ba," sang the sheep, to the tune
of 'Happy birthday to you'.
"Thank you," said Fi, "but I'm not having a
birthday until I find Riff. Have any of you seen
her?"
"Baaa!"

"No? Oh, dear.
Come on, Tom. We'll
have to search the
whole farm," said Fi.

Matt, Mo, Snicker, Wack and Bach decorated the barn for the party.

"Now what else do we need?" wondered Matt.

"No, Wheezy, I don't think Fi wants a gallon of engine oil with her tea. But she will want food. What am I going to do? I know – pizza!"

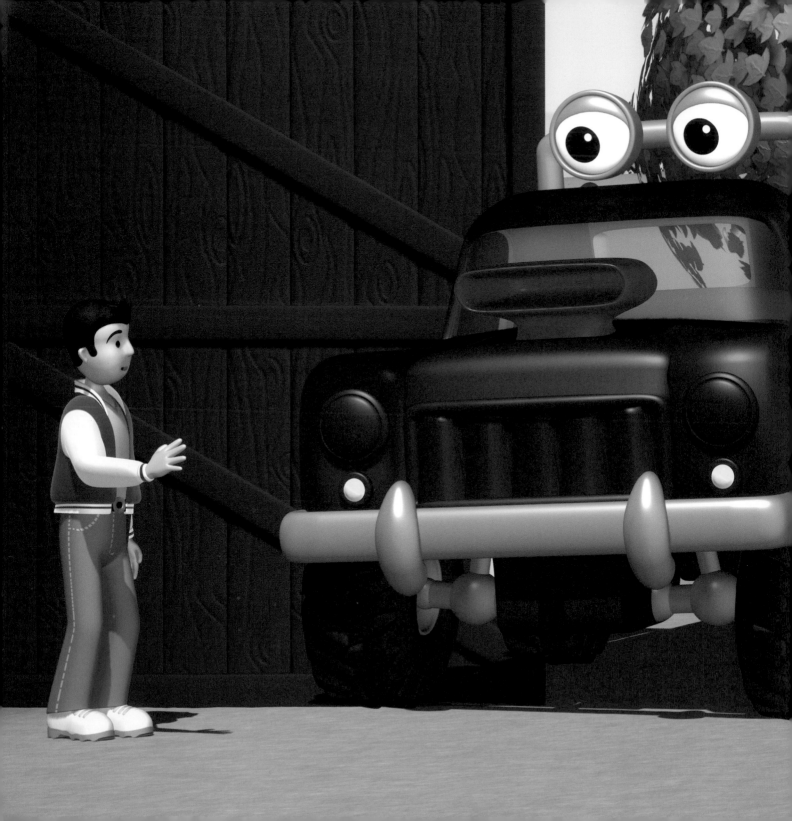

Matt rushed out of the barn to find Rev.

"Rev, I need you to go into Beckton and get take-away pizza for us all.

And remember, no olives for Fi.
And extra cheese for the sheep. Quick as you can," called Matt.

It didn't take Rev long to bring back the pizzas from Beckton. Then disaster struck!

A branch had fallen from a tree and blocked the road. Rev drove straight into it and the pizza flew up into the air! It landed on his windscreen and slid down messily. Oh, dear!

Back at the farm, Matt was wondering
where Rev had got to.

"Can you go and find
him, Buzz?" he asked.
Buzz sped off.

Buzz soon found Rev stuck
behind the fallen branch. He could see that it
was a real emergency... the pizzas were getting
cold! It was a job for Tractor Tom!

Buzz and Rev couldn't move the tree trunk, but it was no trouble for Tom.

On the way back, Tom suddenly thought of one place that Fi hadn't looked for Riff.

Back at Springhill Farm, Fi was feeling very sad.
"This has been the worst birthday I've ever
had," she said.

"Maybe a party would cheer
you up..." suggested Matt.
"No, all I want to do is find
Riff," explained Fi.

Just then, Tom appeared behind
them and swept Fi up onto his forks.
Tom rushed up the hill to the one place where
they hadn't looked for Riff...
Matt's caravan!

When Fi looked inside Matt's caravan she got
a very special surprise.

"That's where Riff was! She was having
puppies!" cried Fi.

"Oh, Riff. They're beautiful!"

"And now we can start your birthday,"
said Matt happily.

"And it'll be extra special
because it's the puppies'
birthday too!" agreed
Farmer Fi.

"Happy birthday, Fi!" said everyone.

There were lots of presents…

From Mo, a pair of gloves to keep Fi's hands warm when she was milking.

The 'Combine Harvester Book of Corny Jokes' from Wheezy…

A quad bike CD player from Buzz.

A big feather duster from Wack and Bach and the hens – made with their own feathers.

A hub cap from Rev.

A new saddle from Snicker and Winnie.

A pot of cream from Purdey.

A new shirt from Matt.

When Fi looked inside Matt's caravan she got a very special surprise.

"That's where Riff was! She was having puppies!" cried Fi.

"Oh, Riff. They're beautiful!"

"And now we can start your birthday," said Matt happily.

"And it'll be extra special because it's the puppies' birthday too!" agreed Farmer Fi.

"Happy birthday, Fi!" said everyone.
There were lots of presents…

From Mo, a pair of gloves to keep Fi's hands warm when she was milking.
The 'Combine Harvester Book of Corny Jokes' from Wheezy…
A quad bike CD player from Buzz.
A big feather duster from Wack and Bach and the hens – made with their own feathers.
A hub cap from Rev.
A new saddle from Snicker and Winnie.
A pot of cream from Purdey.
A new shirt from Matt.

"Thank you, everyone. But I think Tom brought me the best present of all. He found Riff and her puppies!"

"What would we do without him?" laughed Matt.

"What would I do without you all?" smiled Fi.
And everyone cheered happily.

MO

BUZZ

SNICKER

RIFF

WHEEZY

FARMER FI

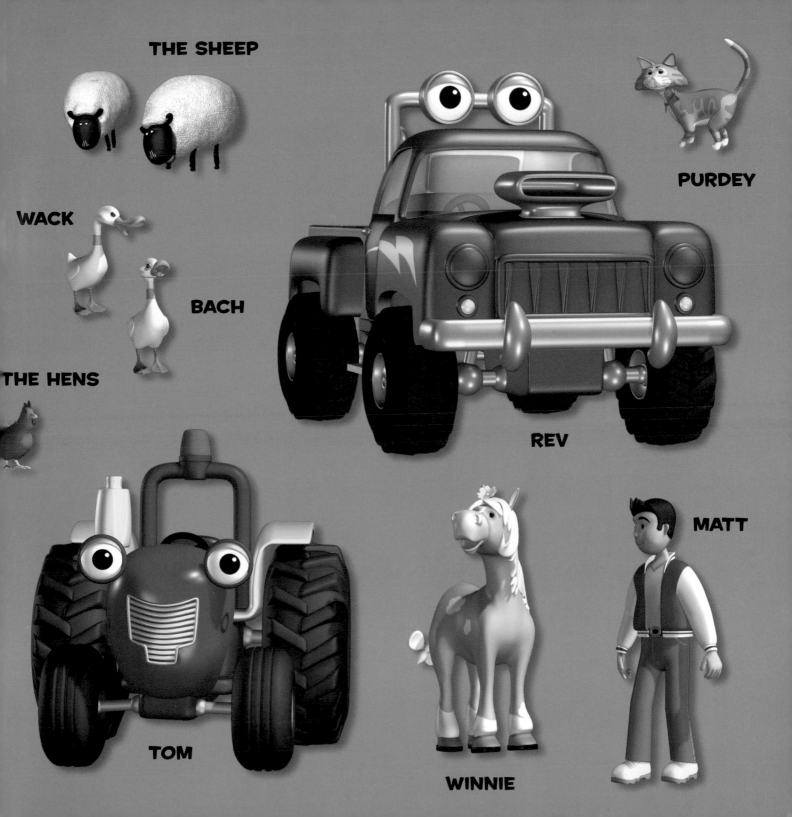

THE SHEEP

PURDEY

WACK

BACH

THE HENS

REV

TOM

WINNIE

MATT

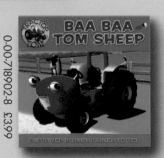